RUSS THOMPSON

TAKEN AWAY

D1073496

Finding Forward

Books

Published by Finding Forward Books. P.O. Box 8182,
Long Beach, CA 90808. www.findingforwardbooks.com.
FF002.27H.2022.07.29.

Editing by Laura Perkins. Series concept by Pam
Sheppard. Cover by Shayne at Wicked Good Book
Covers. Text set in Open Dyslexic Mono.

ISBN: 979-8-6503936-1-0 (Amazon paperback)
ISBN: 978-1-7373157-0-4 (Ingram paperback)

Summary: Miles Pruitt has been struggling in high
school. When his dad is sent to prison, things get
worse. He quits studying, fails classes, and gets
kicked off the basketball team. How will he pick
himself up and move forward?

BISAC Subject Codes: YOUNG ADULT FICTION / Social
Themes / Emotions and Feelings | YOUNG ADULT FICTION
/ Sports and Recreation / Basketball

Lexile measure: HL390L

For Betty-Jean,
our kids,
and grandkids.

CONTENTS

1 GONE

SUNDAY MORNING. The apartment is quiet. Nobody else is up yet.

I turn on the news. I can't believe it.

Lundy's Barbecue caught on fire last night.

Dad works there.

Two firemen climb a ladder onto the roof. They step forward.

The first one punches down on the roof with a long pole.

Smoke pours out.

He steps forward again.

7

The roof caves in.

He falls in with it.

Flames and sparks shoot twenty feet into the air.

I run to my parents' room and bang on the door.

"Dad, wake up! There was a fire at Lundy's last night!"

I rush back to the TV.

Paramedics put the fireman into an ambulance.

Dad comes out of the bedroom.

"Miles, what happened?"

"A fireman fell through the roof. He dropped into the fire."

"What do you mean?"

"It's on the news. He climbed on the roof with another guy. The roof broke. He fell into the fire."

Dad's face turns gray. He runs into the bathroom.

I hear him throw up.

Mom comes into the living room and puts her arm around me.

Abby comes out of her room and holds Mom's hand.

"What happened?" Abby asks.

"There was a fire at Dad's restaurant," Mom says.

The bedroom door opens.

Dad rushes out with his cell phone in his hand.

"I called Mr. Lundy," he says. "I have to get over there."

He hugs Mom and runs out the door.

The TV shows the fireman falling through the roof again.

He took one step and was gone.

2 LIKE A DREAM

FOUR MONTHS LATER. Monday morning.
Mom and Dad ride me to school.

I had hoped this day would never
come.

But it's here.

Dad goes to prison today.

He confessed to setting Lundy's
Barbecue on fire.

Abby cried when we dropped her
off at Longfellow.

She's only ten, a fifth grader,
so I knew she would.

We stop at the curb in front of

Edison High School.

I try to get out.

But I can't move.

Dad gets out and opens the door for me. He has tears in his eyes.

"Miles, don't forget what we talked about," he says. "You have to be strong."

He hugs me with all his strength.

I don't want to let him go.

BASKETBALL COURTS. School starts in forty minutes. Nobody else is here yet.

I miss a short jumper from the right. I grab the rebound and miss another shot.

I also miss the next shot, and the next.

Then it happens.

The tears start.

I try to stop them. But I can't.

I go to the soccer field and sit on a bench where nobody can see me.

He's my dad. I love him.

He's gone.

ENGLISH. My sleeve is still wet from crying. I hope nobody notices.

Ms. Gulliver gives us an article from the Conroy Courier.

I read the words. But they don't mean anything to me.

I look at the others. It's just a regular day to them.

They have no idea what I'm going through.

I remember when Dad told us about the fire.

The owner gave him five-thousand dollars to set it. Nobody was supposed to get hurt.

The lawyer made a deal for Dad to get four years if he pleaded guilty.

With good behavior, he'll be out in two years.

It seems like forever.

HOME. I sit at the kitchen table. All I can do is stare straight ahead.

The door opens. Mom and Abby come in and sit across from me.

Mom reaches out to hold our hands.

"I need both of you to be very strong," she says. "It did not go well in court today."

"What happened?" I ask.

"The judge gave Dad ten years."

It feels like a slap.

I can't believe what she's saying.

"How can that be?" I ask. "The lawyer said Dad would get four years for pleading guilty."

She takes a breath. "The judge gave the maximum sentence because of what happened to the fireman. There were red burn scars all over his face. He was sitting in a wheelchair with a breathing tube stuck down his throat."

Mom cries. "It happened so fast. Dad turned to say goodbye. They led him through a door. He was gone."

I close my eyes and put my head in my hands.

It's like a dream that can't be happening.

3 CAN'T STOP

TUESDAY MORNING. Abby and I walk to school.

I dribble my basketball, trying not to look at it.

"I was waiting for Dad to wake me up this morning," Abby says.

"I know what you mean. I miss him, too."

"Do you think he'll get good behavior?"

"Probably. But even with that, he still won't be out for six years."

My ball hits a crack in the

sidewalk and shoots sideways. I grab it before it reaches the street.

I'm fifteen now. When Dad gets out of prison, I'll be twenty-one.

BASKETBALL COURTS. Before school. I move from side to side, shooting inside jumpers.

None of them go in.

I work on dribbling, using both hands without looking.

The ball hits my foot. I have to run after it.

Tryouts start next week. I won't make it if I don't do better than this.

ENGLISH. Ms. Gulliver comes to the front of the classroom.

"Take out a piece of paper," she says. "Describe a fun experience you've had. Write one page for an A, three-quarters for a B, and half-a-page for a C."

I put the heading on my paper and begin writing.

Miles Pruitt
English 10

Basketball

I remember when Dad would shoot hoops with me. He taught me everything I know.

We would play on Saturdays and Sundays. I wish we could still do it.

Another thing good about Dad is that he liked to tell jokes.

Most of them were stupid. But they were still funny.

He was also good at helping me in math. He knew how to explain it and make it simple.

He used to manage a restaurant, Lundy's Barbecue. They had the best food.

But it's not there anymore.

I finish my half-page. I can get a higher grade if I write more. But I don't feel like it.

I remember the tears on Dad's face when he told us he set the restaurant on fire.

AFTER SCHOOL. Kenny is already at the basketball courts when I get there.

He shoots from the outside, hitting almost everything.

Every time I watch him, I can't

believe how good he is.

I work mostly on my inside shots, missing most of them.

"Miles, you ready to go one-on-one?" Kenny asks.

"Sure."

I bring in the ball and drive past him for a lay-up. It bounces out.

Kenny gets the rebound, takes it back, and hits a three-pointer from the right side.

I get the ball and hit a jumper from the left. But Kenny goes on a scoring run.

He wins the first game, 20-8. He also wins the next one.

We go back to shooting.

"Do you know what prison your dad is going to?" Kenny asks.

I remember when Dad hugged me for

the last time.

It feels like I'm never going to see him again.

I grab the ball and hurl it at the backboard as hard as I can.

I can tell Kenny feels sorry. We continue shooting. I miss another easy shot.

"I never told you," Kenny says. "But I have an uncle in prison."

"What happened?" I ask.

"He was with some guys who robbed a jewelry store."

"How much longer does he have?"

"Two years."

"Where is he?"

"Joplin."

We keep shooting. I miss more shots. We leave to go home.

I can't stop thinking about Dad.

4   GOING BAD

HOME. I walk into the kitchen. Mom turns around. She's been crying.

I reach out to hug her. She holds me tight and cries harder.

I wish I could help her.

"Miles, I'm sorry," she says. "I miss him so much."

"Don't worry," I say. "We're going to get through this."

I look at Dad's chair again. It will be empty for the next six years.

EVENING. I sit at the kitchen table and open the laptop. The hinge is broken, so I have to be careful.

I get on the website of the *Conroy Courier*. A picture on the front page shows Dad walking into the courthouse. Mom walks next to him, staring straight ahead.

Another picture shows the fireman. The scars on his face look like burned leather. The article says he has two kids.

I should be doing my homework now.

But I can't think.

LATER. The laptop sits in front of me. I still haven't done any homework. I click on YouTube.

The first video shows buses pulling into a parking garage at a jail.

Prisoners get off wearing chains on their ankles. I wonder if it was like that for Dad.

The next video shows Joplin State Prison. The cell blocks have guards with rifles.

The warden shows knives that the prisoners made.

One of the inmates has a scar across his face. I wonder if he was slashed with one of those knives.

Mom comes into the kitchen. I don't want her to see the video.

I click off YouTube and go back to my homework.

"How's your math?" she asks.

"I'm still working on it."

"Don't stay up too late."

She leaves. I go back to YouTube. The next video shows a new prisoner who smiles all the time.

The other prisoners call him Gummy Bear. They slap him, push him, and take his food at mealtime.

What if that happens to Dad?

LATER. I open the couch and get under the covers.

I try to sleep. But my mind keeps going in circles.

What's happening to Dad now? What if they think he's weak? What if they decide to jump him?

School is also messed up. I'm behind in history. I also have a big project in English that's due.

I got NoPasses on my tests last week in math and science.

What about Mom? How can I help her get through this?

Everything is going bad.

5 FEEL WORSE

WEDNESDAY MORNING. SCIENCE. I reach
my seat just before the bell rings.

I try not to yawn. I didn't get
much sleep last night.

"Take out your homework," Ms.
Acosta says. "I'll come around and
collect it while you do the warm-up
assignment."

I forgot that today is Wednesday.
I didn't do my homework last night.

If one person in a group doesn't
do it, nobody in the group gets
bonus points.

Ms. Acosta comes to our table. She collects the papers without stamping them with fifty bonus points like she normally does.

Elizabeth glares at me. "Thanks, Miles. You really helped me out."

She has no idea what I'm going through.

MATH. I wish I wasn't here. I hate this class.

Mr. Braden goes to the board.

"This new problem is a little more advanced," he says. "Watch carefully as I go through the steps."

Which item is a better deal? A nine-ounce bag of Flaming Hot Cheetos for $2.98, or six one-ounce bags for $2.28?

I copy what he writes. But I don't understand any of it.

I know I should raise my hand. But the others will think I'm dumb.

Mr. Braden calls for the answer. About ten people raise their hands.

Arturo goes to the board and works it out perfectly.

I watch him closely. But all it does is make me more confused. The next problems don't make sense either.

The bell rings. I slam my book shut. Why am I so stupid?

LUNCH. I reach our table and take out my first sandwich. I'm still upset about math.

Kenny sits down and opens his backpack. "What's wrong?"

"I might have a D in math."

"Do you know about the grade-checks for basketball?" he asks.

"Of course, I know. That's what I'm worried about."

6 CAN'T HELP

EVENING. I set up the laptop on the kitchen table and go to the Edison High website.

First, I do my English. We have to read a current event and describe it in our own words.

I click on the Conroy Courier and choose the first article I see.

I copy sentences from the beginning, middle, and end. That should be good enough.

Science is next. We have a test tomorrow on plants. I open my notebook and glance at the notes.

It's not a big deal. I can study in the morning.

Math. I go to the website and start on the first problem. I don't know how to do it.

I look in my notebook and see the NoPass on my test from yesterday. I tear it up into little pieces.

Abby comes into the kitchen to get a glass of water.

"Miles, why did you tear up your paper?" she asks.

"Don't worry about it."

I look at the website again, copy down the homework problems, and fill in some answers.

I know they're wrong. But at least I'll have something to turn in tomorrow.

LATER. I get on YouTube, put on the headphones, and type Prison Life into the search box.

The first video is about Red Mountain State Prison. It shows a gang fight on the yard. One of the inmates gets stabbed. A guard is beaten.

The next video shows an ex-convict telling how to get along in prison. It has a lot of cussing. He says he was stabbed and beat up.

Something in front of me moves. It's Mom.

"What is that?" she asks. "I can tell you're not doing homework."

I don't want to show her, but I have to. I turn the laptop around so she can see the screen.

"Let me hear it."

I give her the headphones. Her

face turns red.

"Why are you watching this trash?"

"I keep wondering what it's like for Dad."

Her jaw tightens. She looks me in the eye. "Your dad is in jail, not you. There's nothing you can do to help him. He would not want you watching this stuff."

I know she's right. I know I can't help him.

But he's my dad.

7   GOING WRONG

THURSDAY MORNING. Somebody shakes my shoulder. It's Abby.

"Miles, get up. It's after seven."

I look at my alarm clock.

Something went wrong.

It was supposed to go off at six this morning so I could study for the science test today.

I jump into my clothes, run to the kitchen, and pour a bowl of cereal.

I didn't do my science homework

this week. Now, I'm going to get a bad grade on the science test.

SCIENCE. The bell rings. Everybody gets quiet because it's test day.

Ms. Acosta comes to the front of the classroom. "No talking. You get ten minutes to study."

I skim the chapter. Some of it feels like I'm reading it for the first time.

I look at my notes. There's a lot I don't remember.

Ten minutes pass. Ms. Acosta hands out the tests. "Keep your eyes on your own paper. Cover your answers. I'll be watching you."

I look at the first question. I don't know the answer.

I don't know the answers to the second or third questions either.

I shouldn't have watched those videos last night. But it's too late now.

Elizabeth isn't covering up her test paper the way she should.

Nobody in our group likes her. But she's smart.

I copy her first answer, an A. Then I see her answers for the next three questions. I copy those, too.

I didn't think it would be this easy.

I look around the classroom. Ms. Acosta sits at her desk.

I can still see Elizabeth's paper. I copy more answers.

I look up again to check for Ms. Acosta. She's not at her desk.

I feel somebody behind me. It's Ms. Acosta. I'm caught.

She takes my test, marks NoPass

across the front, and continues walking around the room.

Dad is locked up. I'm failing in science.

Everything is going wrong.

8 KEEP SEEING

HOME. I open the front door. Mom
stirs spaghetti on the stove.

I hope Ms. Acosta hasn't called
her.

"Miles, how was school?" she
asks.

"It was fine. Just a regular
day."

"Anything you want to talk
about?"

"Not really," I say. "It was just
a regular day."

Mom's jaw tightens. "Are you

sure?"

"Yes."

The vein on her forehead pops out.

"I got an email from Ms. Acosta. She told me you cheated on your science test."

"The girl next to me didn't cover up her paper. It was an accident."

Mom's hand flies up.

The slap hits me hard.

"Don't ever do that again," she says. "You will not lie and make excuses like your dad."

I know I did wrong. But she didn't have to slap me.

And she didn't have to talk about Dad.

EVENING. I begin the homework for my English class.

We have to write about something memorable.

Miles Pruitt
English 10

Proud of Me

I remember when we used to go to my dad's restaurant. He was the manager of Lundy's Barbecue.

They had the best food. I wish we could still eat there.

I remember when I was ten years old. I found a twenty-dollar bill on the floor.

I gave it to Dad. He said he was proud of me for being honest.

Things are different now. I wish he could be around so I could talk to him.

LATER. Mom comes into the kitchen. She's calm, now. I'm glad when she sits across from me.

"How's your homework?" she asks.

"I got some of it done. I'm sorry for lying."

I give her my English paper. She reads it and smiles.

I'm not sure I should ask. But I decide to, anyway. "Did Dad ever lie to you?"

Her face gets sad. I feel sorry for asking.

"It was hard," Mom says. "The lies got worse and worse. Every time I caught him, he promised he would never do it again."

She reaches out to touch my hand. "I know it's been rough on you. But the bad stuff in life is going to happen. You can't let it bring you down."

That's what's happening. The thing with Dad is bringing me down.

I write the apology letter for Ms. Acosta and put it in my backpack.

I should feel better. But I don't.

I keep seeing Dad in my mind, sitting in a jail cell.

9 WORSE NOW

SATURDAY MORNING. It's still dark. But I can't get back to sleep.

There are a lot of things on my mind.

I wonder what it's like for Dad now. Today will be his sixth day in jail.

I'm glad we get to see him tomorrow. But I don't want to say goodbye to him again.

Basketball tryouts start on Monday. It helps that I'm tall and work hard on defense.

But my shooting is bad. And my ball-handling is weak. There are a lot of guys better than me.

AFTER BREAKFAST. I sit at the kitchen table. What a waste of a Saturday. I'll be doing homework all day.

In English, we have to write an essay about our hardest classes. I finish it in pencil and copy it over in pen.

Miles Pruitt
English 10

My Hardest Classes

My biggest problem now is math. Everybody else understands it. But I don't. I got a NoPass on the test last week.

My other hard class is science. I can understand the work when I do it. But it's boring. I had a low C on the last report card.

In the math test on Wednesday, I didn't know any of it. I looked at my total grade on School View. It's a NoPass.

Basketball tryouts start on Monday. If I make the team, I have to get at least a C in every class.

NOON. I've been working on math for more than two hours.

I'm sick of it. But I have to keep going.

We're working on ratios and proportions. I know I'm making a lot of mistakes.

I wish Dad was here, so he could

help me.

Why did he have to start that
fire?

AFTERNOON. The front door opens. Mom
comes in. "Miles, how's your math?"

"I got eighteen pages done."

"Is it getting any better?"

"Not really."

I picture Dad as I go back to
work. Math was easy for him.

It will never be easy for me.

EVENING. I sit at the kitchen table,
still working on math.

The more I work, the more
confused I get. I don't think any of
it is right.

Mom comes in and sits across from
me.

"How much more do you have?" she

asks.

"This is my last page."

She probably expects me to smile. But how can I be happy when most of it is wrong?

"I'm proud of you for doing this," Mom says. "When I was in school, I had the same problem with math. I should have worked harder."

"What did you do?"

"That's one of the reasons why I didn't go to college. I never did get it."

She leaves the kitchen. I feel worse now.

I've been trying my hardest. But I'll never be good in math.

10 CAN'T QUIT

SUNDAY MORNING. We get off the freeway and turn right. The sign on the street says Vernon County Jail.

I want to see Dad. But I don't want to go inside.

Mom turns right and pulls into the parking structure. I look in the back seat. Abby stares out the side window.

None of us say anything.

We get to the visitors' center and stand in line. I put my hands behind my head and spread my legs apart.

An officer with rubber gloves searches me. He puts his hands everywhere.

I hate him.

A lady officer searches Mom and Abby.

I hate her, too.

ONE HOUR LATER. They call our last name, Pruitt. I get a sick feeling in my stomach.

The officer takes us down a long hallway with booths facing windows.

It's crowded and stuffy. I don't want to be here.

We sit in booth seventeen. Dad comes in and sits across the window from us.

It shocks me to see him wearing an orange prison uniform. He has a purple bruise on the side of his face.

I try to smile. But I can't.

Mom and Dad pick up telephones. I can only hear Mom.

"How are you doing?" she asks. "Did you see a doctor?... Try to be careful... Do you know how much longer you'll be here?"

I watch Dad's face as he talks. His mouth smiles. But his eyes are sad.

Mom gives the phone to Abby.

"I got an A on my math test," Abby says. "And I'm getting an A in history..."

Dad nods his head and tries to smile. I wish we didn't have glass between us.

Abby gives me the phone. My hand shakes. I put it to my ear.

"Miles, how are you doing?" Dad asks.

"Pretty good. Basketball tryouts start tomorrow."

"What do you think?"

"I might have a shot at center. But there are a lot of guys going out."

"What about your classes?"

"Everything is fine."

I know I shouldn't lie. But I don't want him to worry. I can't stop looking at the bruise on his face.

"Dad, did you fall or something?"

"I slipped on the floor and hit my head on a guy's bunk."

I look in his eyes. He's lying.

"What do you do in here?" I ask.

"I read a lot. Sometimes I play cards or dominoes with the guys. I

also do stuff like push-ups and
burpees."

"Do you know how long you'll be
here?"

"I know I'll be going to a
prison. But I don't know when or
where. They just put you on a bus,
and you go."

Mom taps me on the shoulder. I
give her the phone. We take turns
talking.

At thirty minutes, we have to say
goodbye.

Dad puts his hand on the window.
We press our hands to his.

I don't want to go.

EVENING. I open my math folder and
look at my thirty pages of extra
credit.

It was a lot of work. I hope it's

enough.

I begin my science homework. We have to read and answer questions.

Usually, I skim the chapter and copy sentences for the answers.

This time, I read the chapter twice and answer the questions in my own words.

It takes longer, but I feel better about it.

It's late when I finish. I think about the visit with Dad today.

I can't quit seeing the bruise on his face.

11 ONE MORE DAY

MONDAY. MATH. Mr. Braden is gone. We
have a substitute teacher.

I was going to turn in my extra
credit today. This will give me
another night to do more.

AFTER SCHOOL. Basketball tryouts.
Kenny and I walk into the gym.

The other guys are already
warming up. It's hard not to be
nervous.

I pick up a ball, shoot from the
side, and miss. I take another shot

and miss that one, too.

I look to the side. Kenny makes a three-pointer. He's the best guy out here. I know he'll make it.

Coach Reed blows his whistle. "Gentlemen, to the bleachers."

I sit in the front and glue my eyes on Coach Reed. He may be an English teacher, but he seems more like a drill sergeant.

"There are twenty-four of you," he says. "We have fifteen spots. The first cut is today. The final cut is tomorrow. We have a practice game against Hamilton on Thursday."

He paces back and forth in front of us. I notice the scar on his chin. I wonder how he got it.

"There are three things that count in life," he says. "Tell the truth, work hard, and never give up.

If you make this team, you will promise to give your best effort during every minute of practice."

"You will also work hard in your classes," he says. "If you make the team, you will turn in a grade-check every Thursday. You will not play in any game unless you have a C or higher in every class."

The grade-checks worry me. I have to bring up my math grade.

BASKETBALL FLOOR. Coach Reed places us into four groups.

One of the guys in my group is Donny. I don't like him.

He used to laugh at me and slap the back of my head in grade school.

He's tall, like me. But he's much stronger.

He also plays dirty.

"The first drill is dribbling,"
Coach Reed says. "Go downcourt and
back. Keep your eyes up. Switch
hands when you get to each cone."

I get the ball and dribble
forward. It hits my foot and bounces
to the side.

I run for the ball and see Coach
Reed frowning at me.

Next, we have defensive drills. I
go full speed, stay low, and keep my
arms out.

"Good job," Kenny says.

On shooting drills, I miss all
three shots. One of them is an
airball.

I look to the side and see Donny
laughing.

The harder I try, the worse I
get.

Rebounding comes next. I fight

for position, jump, and grab the first rebound.

Donny elbows me in the ribs when I go for the second one. But I cut in front of him and still get it.

I pull down four rebounds. Donny gets one. It feels good to beat him.

Next, we line up for suicides. Coach Reed blows his whistle.

We run from the end line to the free-throw line and back, to the half-court line and back, to the far free-throw line and back, and to the far end-line and back. That's one suicide.

Everybody runs hard at first. By the third suicide, some guys slow down.

But not me.

I've been working hard on my running since last spring.

By the fifth suicide, I'm in sixth place. By the tenth, I'm in third. Kenny gets first. Donny comes in last.

We go back to our groups and shoot free-throws. I make four of fifteen. Donny makes eleven.

Coach Reed blows his whistle. I walk slowly to the locker room.

I did okay on defense and rebounding.

But I choked on everything else.

I don't think I'm going to make it.

LOCKER ROOM. I finish dressing and sit on the bench in front of my locker.

The cut list is up. A bunch of guys crowd around looking at it.

I tie my shoes slowly. I don't

want to see it.

"Don't count yourself out," Kenny says. "You were super on defense and rebounding. Plus, you did great on suicides."

We get up and look at the list. It has twenty names on it.

Kenny made it. Donny made it.

Then I see my name, Miles Pruitt.

We have one more day of tryouts. Maybe things are getting better.

Maybe I can make the team.

12 WRECKING IT

TUESDAY. MATH. Mr. Braden is absent again.

I'll do five more pages of extra credit tonight.

I hope we don't have a test tomorrow.

AFTER SCHOOL. Basketball floor. I'm as nervous as I was yesterday.

Coach Reed stands in front of us. "The name of this drill is threes. Three guys on offense. Three on defense."

"You'll play fast break and full-court press until I blow the whistle," he says. "Then the next two teams will go in."

He reads off the names. I'm on team five. Kenny goes to team six, with Donny.

This is my last chance.

If I choke, I'm out.

Teams one and two begin. They go full out for six minutes. Teams three and four go in after them.

My team is next.

I try to relax.

We run onto the floor. Donny smiles like he thinks he's going to beat me.

I try not to look at him.

Kenny throws the ball in. They bring it downcourt. The ball goes to Donny on the right side.

I stay low on him with my arms out. He can't get around me.

I try to knock the ball out of his hands.

Donny passes. I tip it out of bounds.

Kenny passes the ball to Donny.

Donny can't get a shot over me and passes outside. Kenny puts it up but misses.

Donny elbows me in the ribs and jumps for the rebound. I elbow him back and leap sideways to grab it.

Donny jams down on the ball. It hits me in the jaw and flies out to Kenny. He shoots and scores a three-pointer.

We bring the ball downcourt. I cross under the basket to get open.

Donny trips me. I fall. The ball bounces off the rim.

Donny grabs the rebound. He fires the ball to Kenny, who races upcourt to make a lay-up.

We're behind 5-0. We bring the ball downcourt. I put up a short jumper and miss.

Donny elbows me. I push around him to get position. I leap for the rebound.

Donny rams his shoulder into my back. I go down again.

The ball flies to Kenny. He takes it upcourt. Donny gets open inside.

Kenny passes to him. Donny scores. They go ahead 7-0.

Coach Reed whistles. We're done.

There's no way I'm going to make the team, now.

LOCKER ROOM. Kenny and I get dressed. I try not to show how I feel.

"Donny was playing you pretty hard," Kenny says. "But you didn't let him beat you."

"He cheated. He's a dirty player. And Coach Reed didn't see it."

"Maybe Coach Reed wanted to find out how tough you were," Kenny says. "You kept coming back on Donny, even when he knocked you down."

I take my time dressing. Kenny is wrong. It's all over for me.

Everybody else is gone by the time we look at the cut list.

I see Kenny's name. I knew it would be there.

Then, near the bottom, I see Miles Pruitt.

I put my finger under my name and read it again.

I wish I could tell Dad.

"Guess what?" Kenny says. "I don't see Donny's name."

HOME. I sit at the kitchen table. I have to do three more pages of extra credit for math.

Mom comes in and sits across from me. "When do your games start?"

"This Thursday. We play Hamilton."

"You don't seem very excited," she says.

"We're having grade-checks. I'm not so sure about math."

I'm happy I made the team. But math is wrecking it.

13 ONLY CHANCE

WEDNESDAY. MATH. I give Mr. Braden
my extra credit.

"Miles, what's this?" he asks.

"It's forty pages. I made the
basketball team. We have grade-
checks tomorrow."

"You think I'm going to check
this by tomorrow?"

"Please?"

He tosses it on his desk like I'm
wasting his time.

It makes me feel like nothing.

He comes to the front of the

classroom. Everybody gets quiet.

"You're getting a break today because I've been absent," he says. "The test will be on the same kind of problems you had last week. You should be fine if you've been doing your homework."

I have been doing my homework. But it hasn't helped me.

I know I'm going to fail.

He hands out the tests. All of the questions are word problems. The first one is about cars and gas mileage.

I have no idea what to do.

The other problems are the same.

I can't do them, either.

My only chance to get a C on the grade-check tomorrow is if my extra credit is good enough.

AFTER SCHOOL. Basketball floor.
Practice starts in ten minutes. We
shoot around for warm-ups.

I feel like I belong now.

The position chart says I'll be
playing second-team center.

Coach Reed blows his whistle.
"Have a seat in the bleachers."

He stands silently and looks at
us. I feel important when he makes
eye contact with me.

"This is a fact," he says. "Out
of all the guys who tried out, you
were the best. It wasn't just about
your skills. It was also about your
hard work."

"You made this team because of
your heart," he says. "You worked
hard before tryouts to make your
skills better. You hustled on
defense. You kept going on suicides,

even when you were dead tired.
That's what I mean by heart."

"Always remember this," he says.
"You can do anything if you set your
mind to it and work hard. Make up
your mind that you will not let
anything stop you from reaching your
goals."

I feel ten feet tall.

I will do everything full speed,
all the way, with all my heart.

Maybe I'll get to play in the
Hamilton game tomorrow.

HOME. Dinner is over. I set up the
laptop on the kitchen table.

History is first. I read the
pages carefully and answer the
questions in my own words.

It takes forty minutes. But I
feel good because I did it right.

Next is science. I do it the same way, reading and answering the questions carefully.

I'm tired when I finish. But I'm not going to cut corners anymore.

It's eight o'clock when I start math. I do my best. But most of my answers are guesses.

If Dad was here, he could help me. I can't ask Mom because she's terrible in math.

Coach Reed told us to work hard and never give up.

Maybe it will help if I do ten more pages of extra credit and give it to Mr. Braden in the morning.

I go back to the math website and do more problems.

They're probably wrong. But at least Mr. Braden will know I tried.

TEN O'CLOCK. Mom comes into the kitchen. "How are you doing?"

"I finished five pages. I'm trying to get at least ten."

"You won't be able to think tomorrow if you don't get enough sleep," she says. "You also have your game tomorrow."

"I know. But I have to finish ten pages. That's my only chance to get a C on the grade-check."

14 DOESN'T HELP

THURSDAY MORNING. Abby and I walk to school. I dribble my basketball.

"Miles, why are you yawning?" she asks.

"I had a lot of homework. I stayed up late last night."

"Why are you wearing a tie to school?"

"Everybody on the team has to. The coach wants us to look good on game days."

We get to the corner and turn right.

It won't matter how I look if I don't get a C in math today.

BEFORE SCHOOL. I wait outside Mr. Braden's room.

He's in a rush when he finally gets there. I give him the extra credit.

"You did more?" he asks.

"It's ten pages. I thought it would help."

"I'll check it," he says. "But your grade on the test yesterday also matters."

He hurries into the room and closes the door.

He didn't seem mad like he was yesterday. Maybe I have a chance.

MATH. Mr. Braden walks around the classroom and returns our test papers from yesterday.

I got C's on my grade-checks in English, history, and science. I know I'll get good grades in PE and art.

All I need is a C in math.

Mr. Braden comes to my desk. I get my test back, a D.

It's a setback. But I still have a chance.

My overall grade-check for basketball is what really matters.

Class starts. I pay attention and try my hardest.

But it's like it always is. I can't understand the way Mr. Braden teaches.

There's a minute left when he returns my grade-check.

I hold my breath.

It's a D.

I tried my hardest. But it wasn't good enough.

"Your extra credit helped," Mr. Braden says. "You brought up your grade from a NoPass."

"But I can't play with a D."

"If you come early tomorrow, we can talk about it," he says.

"But our game is today."

"You need to come tomorrow."

The bell rings. I run from the classroom, ball up the grade-check, and throw it in the trash can.

I rip off my tie and jam it in my pocket.

All my work was for nothing.

LUNCH. I don't want to talk to Kenny. I don't want anyone to see me.

I walk to the soccer field and

sit alone on the bleachers.

I'm off the team. There's nothing I can do about it. I'll never be good in math.

HOME. I open the front door. Mom and Abby aren't here yet. I take off my backpack and slam it on the floor.

It's almost dark when Mom and Abby get home. Abby goes into her room. Mom sits next to me on the couch.

"What happened?" she asks.

"I got a D in math."

"What about all the extra work you did?"

"It wasn't good enough."

She puts her arm around my shoulder. It doesn't help.

Basketball is over for me.

15 DIDN'T THINK

FRIDAY MORNING. Abby and I walk to school.

I wanted to stay home. But Mom wouldn't let me.

"How come you don't have your basketball?" Abby asks.

"I don't need it anymore."

"What if your grade comes up?"

"That's not going to happen."

We get to the corner and turn right. She has no idea what I'm going through.

ENGLISH. Ms. Gulliver passes out a news article.

"This is about a soldier who lost his legs in the war," she says. "Now he races wheelchairs and works at a counseling center for veterans. That makes him a champion, to get knocked down and keep trying."

I know Ms. Gulliver wants to help us. That's why she gives us these articles.

But I've already been trying my hardest. It's not as easy as she thinks it is.

HISTORY. Mr. Rubio gives me a blue slip to see my counselor.

I don't know why. Ms. Chang has never sent for me before.

I get to her office. Coach Reed is also there. Now, I'm really confused.

"Miles, what happened yesterday?" Coach Reed asks.

"I got a D in math."

"Why didn't you come and tell me?"

"I didn't think it would matter. I knew I was off the team."

"Don't you want to come back?"

"I'm trying to do better. But when my dad got arrested, everything fell apart. I can't bring up my grade in math."

"Did you talk to your teacher?" Coach Reed asks.

"I gave Mr. Braden all kinds of extra credit. But he said it wasn't good enough."

"When you go to math today, ask Mr. Braden if you can talk to him after school," Coach Reed says. "Let him know everything that's going on. Ask him for help."

"You don't know him like I do. He's not going to care."

"I think you'll be surprised," Ms. Chang says. "Sometimes people seem hard on the outside. But that's not how they are on the inside."

They don't know Mr. Braden. He's not going to help me.

"Do you remember what I said about never giving up?" Coach Reed asks. "Part of that means asking for help when you need it. If you want to get better, you have to ask Mr. Braden for help."

"Am I off the team?"

"You're on probation. As soon as you have a C in everything, you can start practicing again."

The bell rings. I leave for my

science class.

I never thought Coach Reed would send for me. I didn't think he would care.

I'll talk to Mr. Braden. But I don't think it will change anything.

16 MAYBE

FRIDAY AFTERNOON. I walk to Mr.
Braden's room when school gets out.

It's not going to help me. But I
said I would go.

His door is open when I get
there. Some other students sit at
the front.

I sit in the chair next to his
desk at the back of the room.

"Miles, you may not think so,"
Mr. Braden says. "But I felt bad
when I gave you that D."

I didn't expect this. He seems

Like a different person, now that he's talking to me by myself.

"I've been trying to get better," I say. "But I can't understand how to do the word problems."

"What's happening with basketball?" he asks.

"I'm on probation. I missed the game yesterday. I can't get back on the team unless I bring up my math grade."

He types something into his computer and turns the screen toward me. I see my name and a lot of numbers.

"This is from School View," he says. "It shows your scores back to grade school. Your reading scores are fine. But your math scores show you've been weak since the third grade."

"Math has always been hard for me. I didn't think there was much I could do about it."

"Let me show you the Khan Academy," Mr. Braden says. "It's a website with videos on how to do math."

He gets on his web browser and types in Khan Academy. A lesson comes up about the ratio of apples to oranges.

It's the same thing we worked on during class today.

A man with a calm voice explains how to solve the problem. He also draws pictures on the screen showing what to do.

"What do you think?" Mr. Braden asks.

"That Khan guy makes it seem easy. I can understand what he's talking about."

Mr. Braden watches while I do the lesson. It takes twenty minutes.

Next, there's a test. I get five out of the seven questions right.

"Do you have a computer at home?" he asks.

"We have a laptop."

"I want you to get on the Khan Academy at home and work on these lessons," he says. "I'll keep track of what you do from my computer. If you finish all the work and get at least a C on the test next Wednesday, I'll give you a C on your grade-check."

I thought it was all over for me.

But now, I have a chance.

Mr. Braden isn't so bad after all.

EVENING. I turn on the laptop and get on the Khan Academy.

I go to the second lesson and begin. I take the quiz and get all the answers right.

Mom comes into the kitchen. "I never thought I would see you doing homework on a Friday night."

"Mr. Braden gave me twenty-six lessons to finish by next Wednesday."

"You seem excited."

"I'm doing this thing called the Khan Academy. I think it's helping me."

Maybe I can do it.

Maybe I can get back on the team.

17   NEVER FELT

SATURDAY MORNING. We finish breakfast. I set up the laptop on the kitchen table.

Mom comes in and pours herself a cup of coffee. "How late did you stay up last night?"

"Until eleven."

She sits down next to me. "How does this academy thing work?"

"A guy named Khan writes out the problems on the computer screen as he tells you what to do. If you don't understand it the first time, you can watch it again."

Mom sips her coffee.

"It's helping me," I say. "For the first time in math, I feel like I'm learning. Every time I finish a lesson and take the test, it shows up on Mr. Braden's computer. He's keeping track of me."

I go to the next lesson and begin. Mom watches. I show her what to do. It makes me feel smart.

"I'm glad you found this," Mom says. "During all my years in school, math was always my worst subject. This would have helped me."

AFTER LUNCH. I work on the Khan Academy. I'm tired, but I feel like I'm learning.

Mom's phone rings. I wonder who she's talking to.

"Miles, it's your Dad!"

I jump up and run to the living room. She gives me the phone. I'm excited to hear Dad's voice.

"Miles, I need to talk to you."

He sounds mad, like I did something wrong.

"Mom told me you got kicked off the basketball team," Dad says. "What's going on?"

"I got a D in math. But my teacher is helping me now. I'm finally starting to get it."

"Mom also said you were watching prison videos."

"I was worried about you. She told me to stop watching, and I did."

"I don't want you to know what prison is like," Dad says. "I'm locked up. I don't like it. But I'm going to get through it."

I remember the bruise on his face. I wonder what really happened.

"I didn't want to tell you," Dad says. "But a guy tried to punk me before you guys came to visit. He bumped me and did it on purpose to see what I would do."

"I had to stand up to him," Dad says. "That's how I got banged up. The other guy got banged up, too. Nobody else has bothered me since then."

I picture Dad socking the guy. It makes me feel less worried.

"I'm telling you this because I don't want you to worry about me," Dad says. "Now let me talk to your sister. I only have five minutes left."

Abby takes the phone and begins

talking.

I feel better about things. Dad sounds like he's going to be okay.

LATE AFTERNOON. I work on the Khan Academy. Mom comes into the kitchen and sits across from me.

"What lesson are you on?" she asks.

"Number seven."

"How is it?"

"I never thought I would feel smart in math. Now, I'm starting to."

She leaves. I go back to the Khan Academy.

It's a lot of work. But I understand it now.

I've never felt this way about math before.

18 ALL I HAD

MONDAY MORNING. Library, before school. I take out the review sheet for science and look at my notes.

I've never felt so ready for a test before.

I spent hours studying. But I want to do a little more.

The room is warm. I stand up and stretch so I don't nod off.

ENGLISH. Ms. Gulliver comes to the front.

I get sleepy again and sit up

straight.

"A lot of people have the mistaken belief that college is only for some people," she says. "It's important for you to know that college is for everybody."

She points to the college chart on her bulletin board.

"You go step by step, grade by grade," she says. "If you're successful in grade ten, you'll be ready for grade eleven. If you're successful in grade twelve, you'll be ready for grade thirteen."

"And it doesn't have to be a four-year college," she says. "It can be a community college, career training, or the military. They are all good."

Our assignment is to write about our goals after high school.

Now that I'm doing better in math, I have a lot of possibilities.

SCIENCE. I think I have a chance to get an A on the test today.

Ms. Acosta comes to the front of the classroom. "No talking. You have ten minutes to study."

I open my book and skim the chapter. I know it perfectly.

The room is warm. I'm a little sleepy. I sit up straight and open my eyes wide.

Ms. Acosta hands out the tests. "You have twenty-four multiple-choice questions and one essay. The essay is worth twenty-five percent of your grade. Keep your eyes on your own paper. You may put your head down when you finish."

I start the first question. It's

easy. So is the next one.

I finish the multiple-choice section with no problems.

The essay question is next. I put my head down to rest before I begin.

It's been a lot of work. But it's been worth it. I picture myself back on the basketball team.

There's tapping on my shoulder.

I open my eyes.

Ms. Acosta is collecting the tests.

I fell asleep. I didn't finish the last section.

I'll probably get a D. All I had to do was stay awake.

MATH. Mr. Braden stands at the door.

"Miles, I saw your work on the Khan Academy," he says. "Great job."

It's nice of him to say that. But

it doesn't really matter.

I won't be able to play since I'll be getting a D in science.

Mr. Braden turns on the PowerPoint and shows us the first problem.

If Marcus can ride his bike 10 miles in 45 minutes, how long will it take him to ride 12 miles?

"This is similar to a question you'll have on the test tomorrow," Mr. Braden says. "Get started."

I find the answer and raise my hand. Mr. Braden waits while some others finish.

"Miles," he says. "What's the answer?"

"Fifty-four minutes."

"Very good. Come to the front and

show us."

I feel everybody watching me as I walk to the front. I've never done a problem on the board before.

They're going to be surprised to see what I can do.

LUNCH. I take out my sandwich. Kenny sits across from me.

"What are you so down about?" he asks.

"I won't be coming back to the team this week. I fell asleep during my science test. I'll probably be getting a D on my grade check."

I worked so hard. All I had to do was stay awake.

19 GLAD I DIDN'T

TUESDAY MORNING. Abby and I walk to
school. I dribble my basketball as
we walk.

"Miles, do you think you can get
back on the team?" Abby asks.

"Not right away. Ms. Acosta
doesn't accept extra credit. And
we're not having another test until
two weeks from now."

"Why are you taking your
basketball to school?"

"In two weeks, we'll have six
games left. I'll still have a chance

to play if I can get my grades up by then."

SCIENCE. Ms. Acosta frowns as she returns the tests from yesterday.

I can tell by their faces that a lot of people are getting bad grades. I know I'm going to be one of them.

Ms. Acosta comes to my desk. I'm ready to get a D. But when I look at the grade, it's a C.

I got zero points on the essay. But I got a perfect score on the multiple-choice questions.

My work paid off. I still have a chance to get back on the team this week.

MATH. I studied hard for the test today. I shouldn't be nervous. But I am.

"You'll have sixteen problems, including four word-problems," Mr. Braden says. "Good luck."

My heart pounds as he passes out the tests. I look at the first problem.

I know how to do it. I glance at the other ones. They're just like the review sheet.

It's ten minutes early when I finish. I check my answers again. I'm pretty sure I got all of them right.

I thought it was hopeless. I never thought I could be good in math.

If things work out, I'll be back on the team this week. I'm glad I didn't throw my tie away.

20 REED'S WORDS

THURSDAY MORNING. SCIENCE. Ms.
Acosta frowns when she sees my
grade-check.

But when she fills in the grade,
it's a C.

"Miles, you're four points from a
D," she says. "You have a lot of
work to do."

MATH. Mr. Braden smiles. My grade
from him is a C.

It happened. It's real. I'm back
on the team.

LOCKER ROOM. I stand in line to get my uniform. Coach Reed smiles when he sees my grade-check.

I sit next to Kenny and get dressed for the game. I wish I wasn't so nervous.

"Franklin has a center who might be the best in the league," Kenny says. "I've known him since fourth grade."

"What about Wendell?" I say. "He's good."

"This guy from Franklin is better," Kenny says. "When you get in there, you have to go hard on him. Don't let him get the ball."

I'm glad to be back on the team. But what if I mess up? I close my eyes and tell myself to breathe slower.

PREGAME. We run onto the court. I see Mom and Abby in the stands.

Mr. Braden sits near them. I never thought I would see him at a game.

We finish warm-ups and gather around Coach Reed.

"Play tough defense and go hard on the boards," he says. "Keep the ball moving and make smart passes."

The buzzer sounds. I sit on the bench as the starters go in.

FIRST HALF. Wendell wins the tip-off.

Kenny dribbles the ball downcourt and passes to Wendell under the basket. The Franklin center knocks it out of Wendell's hands.

We trade baskets with Franklin but can't get ahead.

Two minutes left in the first quarter. Coach Reed puts me in. Wendell needs a rest.

I go full speed, grabbing a rebound and almost blocking a shot. The Franklin center elbows me in the side.

I keep my arms out, move quickly, and stop the ball from reaching him. My hard work on defense is paying off.

Second quarter. Wendell comes in. We continue to trade baskets with Franklin.

We're behind 24-20 when we run into the locker room for halftime.

"Remember what I told you about wearing them down," Coach Reed says. "Don't let up. That's how we're going to win."

SECOND HALF. Wendell drives in and scores on a reverse lay-up. Kenny scores twice. We inch ahead 32-30.

Fourth quarter. We're two points behind. Kenny misses a jumper from the right.

Wendell goes up for the rebound and gets it. He comes down sideways on his ankle and falls to the floor.

He's hurt. It looks like a bad sprain.

"Miles, get in there," Coach Reed says.

Three minutes left. Franklin is ahead 38-36. We have to score.

I stay on the center as hard as I can. He brings down a rebound and goes up for a shot.

I jump to block it. I miss. The ball goes in. We're down 40-36.

Coach Reed calls a time-out. The

scoreboard shows a minute left.

"This is it," he says. "Get the ball to Kenny."

The crowd roars. I look in the stands. Abby jumps up and down. Mr. Braden pumps his fist in the air.

Kenny brings the ball up, fakes left, and shoots. The ball goes in for a three-pointer.

Thirty seconds left. We're behind 40-39. Coach Reed calls our last time-out.

"Take the ball away," he says. "All we need is one good shot."

Franklin brings the ball in. Kenny steals it.

I race downcourt. I'm under the basket.

Kenny passes the ball to me.

This is my chance.

I go up for an easy bank shot.

The ball hits the rim. It bounces sideways.

I missed.

Franklin gets the rebound. The buzzer sounds.

I blew it.

LOCKER ROOM. I sit on the bench with my head down. We lost because I choked.

Coach Reed sits down next to me. "I know you feel bad. But you showed a lot of heart. You brought up your grades. And you played hard today. I'm proud of you."

I finish dressing. I still feel bad about losing.

But Coach Reed's words mean a lot to me.

21 FORWARD NOW

TWO WEEKS LATER. Monday morning. I
eat breakfast with Mom and Abby.

"What's the name of the prison
where they sent Dad?" Abby asks. "I
keep forgetting."

"Joplin," Mom says.

"When do you think we can go
there?"

"Maybe next weekend. I have to
plan it out since it's so far away.
We'll have to stay overnight
somewhere."

It scares me that Dad is at

Joplin. I remember the video I saw, and how the prisoners beat up one of the guards.

It's also the prison where Kenny's uncle is at.

I'll never feel good until Dad is home. It's going to be six long years.

BASKETBALL COURTS. School starts in thirty minutes.

I dribble right and hit a shot from the free-throw line.

Kenny grabs the ball and makes a jumper from the left.

I get the ball and bank it in from under the basket.

It's the same shot I missed two weeks ago when we played Franklin.

"Miles, how's your dad doing?" Kenny asks.

"They moved him to Joplin. It just happened."

"I talked to my aunt after you told me about the video," Kenny says. "My uncle has never had a problem there. The video you saw was ten years old."

I hit a shot from the right. Maybe Joplin won't be so bad.

MATH. Mr. Braden gives us a review sheet for the test this week.

The problems are easy. I know what I'm doing because I've been working on the Khan Academy every night.

Mr. Braden walks over and kneels next to me. "I'm going to move your seat next to Arthur tomorrow. See if you can help him. I think he's getting discouraged."

It makes me feel good that Mr. Braden has faith in me. After all my troubles, I never thought I would be asked to help someone else in math.

DINNER. We're having tacos tonight. Mom and Abby sit down.

"There was a story in the newspaper about the fireman who was burned," Mom says. "He's walking now. He's done with his surgeries."

I'm so glad to know he's getting better.

I will always feel terrible about what happened to him.

EVENING. I get on the laptop and type Raymond State College into the search box.

The website has pictures of the campus and a list of majors. It's one of the colleges I've been thinking about.

Coach Reed told us to work hard and never give up.

Mom said to think about the future and not let the bad stuff get to me.

It hasn't been easy. I've been through a lot. But I feel like it's going to be okay.

I feel like I'm moving forward now.

ACKNOWLEDGMENTS

I am very grateful to the many people who gave me feedback while I was writing this book.

FAMILY AND FRIENDS: Allison Alomair, Shannon Bayatpur, Gloria Bill, Ron Connor, Genni Contrades, Carol Fowler, Shirley Howard, Ed Kamiyama, and Bob Thompson.

COFFEE HOUSE WRITERS GROUP: John Arfwedson, Christopher Dane, Clyde Fugami, Samantha Hancox-Li, Paul James, J. Bryan Jones, Alex Khansa, Phil Levy, John Lowell, Neora Luria, Dollie Mason, Scott McClelland, Viet Nguyen, Dav Pauli, Jean Pliska, Diego Ramirez, AnneLise Wilhelmsen, and Dennis Wolverton.

SOUTHERN CALIFORNIA WRITERS ASSOCIATION: Annie Moose, Pam Sheppard, and Janis Thomas.

SOUTHERN CALIFORNIA WRITERS CONFERENCE: Robert Golino, Ara Grigorian, Melanie Hooks, Jean Jenkins, Laura Perkins, John Rudolph, and Claudia Whitsitt.

SOCIETY OF CHILDREN'S BOOK WRITERS AND ILLUSTRATORS: Tim Burke, Erzsi Deak, Christine Henderson, Linda Ruddy, Lorian Steider Brady, Teri Vitters, Janet Youngdahl, Kim McClinton, Bev Plass, Scott Sussman, and Jesper Widen.

I wish to thank Laura Perkins and Pam Sheppard for their wisdom and careful editing.

Thank you, Betty-Jean, for your patience, your suggestions, your Love, and for being my wife.

ABOUT THE AUTHOR

 My dream of becoming a writer started at Whitworth University. I was lucky to have a teacher, Dr. Tammy Reid, who believed in me and encouraged me. After college, I began a career as an educator, teaching reading and English at a middle school in Los Angeles. I later served as a high-school principal. During my many years of working with young people, I observed that every student can succeed. If you can dream it, you can achieve it. Set your sights high, work hard every day, and don't let anything keep you from achieving your dreams.

ADDITIONAL TITLES

NO PLACE TO HIDE. Owen Daniels, now in his first year of high school, battles to overcome a serious reading problem. He must also learn to believe in himself.

NEVER WANTED. Roy Perkins never knew his dad, his mom died in a meth-lab explosion, and his alcoholic uncle beats him. He is sent to live with a caring foster family. But the challenges continue.

ALL ALONE. Tenth grader Elgin Hobbs seems fine on the outside. But he's failing classes, his divorced parents fight, and his mom is an alcoholic. How can he rise above these troubles and keep going?

CPSIA information can be obtained
at www.ICGtesting.com
Printed in the USA
BVHW042059131022
649111BV00002B/14

9 781737 315704